RAPunzel
A HAPPENIN' RAP

By
David Vozar

Illustrated by
Betsy Lewin

A Doubleday Book for Young Readers

A Doubleday Book for Young Readers
Published by
Bantam Doubleday Dell Publishing Group, Inc.
1540 Broadway
New York, New York 10036
Doubleday and the portrayal of an anchor with a dolphin are trademarks of
Bantam Doubleday Dell Publishing Group, Inc.

Library of Congress Cataloging-in-Publication Data
Vozar, David.
    Rapunzel : a happenin' rap / by David Vozar ; illustrated by Betsy Lewin.
       p.   cm.
    Summary: A take-off, in rap style, on the story of a girl with long hair who
is imprisoned by a witch.
    ISBN 0-385-32314-X (alk. paper)
    [1. Fairy tales.   2. Folklore.   3. Stories in rhyme.] I. Lewin, Betsy, ill.
II. Title.
    PZ8.3.V898Rap 1998
    398.2—dc20   96-35361
                                                                          CIP
                                                                          AC
    The text of this book is set in 14.5- point Century Old Style.
            Book design by Trish Parcell Watts
        Manufactured in the United States of America
                      March 1998
            10 9 8 7 6 5 4 3 2 1

This book is dedicated to family . . .

my mom and pop,

Mark, Amy, Laura, and Sarah,

and my daughter, Ariane.

—D.V.

In memory of L. Frank Baum.

—B.L.

The *Hair-Raising* Beginning

Here's a tale 'bout the girl with long locks,
Lived not far from here, maybe four blocks.
You may think you already know what happened,
But you'll know more after hearing my rapping.

It started when this man and his wife
Were living small in hunger and strife.
They were expecting their first baby to come
When the daddy-to-be did something real dumb.

He went to buy marshmallow ice cream.
Bought a big scoop and in a daydream,
He was thinking up some names for his child
When he bumped into someone outrageously wild.

His ice cream went flying and spilled out.
The guy looked up when he heard a shout.
It was the bad witch from the building next door,
Now covered in goo like a humongous s'more.

The folks in the hood knew she was mean,
The evilest witch they'd ever seen.
And now she was angry, crinkled up her nose,
As the man reached up, started wiping her clothes.

The witch said, "Stop fussing. Tell me now,
Would you like to be a newt or a cow?"
The shocked man said, "I'm sorry! Please don't zap me!
My wife is pregnant. I'll soon be a pappy."

She said, "Off with you! Out of my face!"
The dude ran home as if in some race.
Witch followed behind him 'cause she was still mad,
To snatch his new baby and make him feel bad.

His daughter was born later that day.
The witch appeared and said, "Now you'll pay."
She pointed her wand and *zap!* came a bright light.
"Say good-bye, baby . . . and to all a good night!"

Witch whisked Rapunzel to a building so rare
With one high window, no door and no stairs.
Up, up, went the baby, to the highest room,
Where no one would find her. You'd think she was doomed.

Baby Rapunzel grew up to a girl—
After six years had a full head of curls.

Rapunzel, the girl, grew up to a teen—
Her curls grew faster than you've ever seen.

Rapunzel, the teen, grew up so fair—
But now she had more than ten feet of hair

The Locked-Up Rapunzel

Witch spent all her time pleasing Rap.
All Rap wanted, the witch would just *zap!*
She zapped braces for Rap's crooked molars.
When Rap wanted curls, *Zap!* appeared rollers.

But Rapunzel soon wanted "More! More!"
Whining and whining from noon to four.
She whined for a TV and radio.
She whined to have pizza made to go.

She whined for all the latest teen mags.
A new wardrobe— "My stuff is all rags.
I must have the newest designer wear."
The witch grew tired. Rap didn't care.

One day Witch said, "Enough is enough!
I'm tuckered out from zapping you stuff.
I'm out of here, Toots. You're on your own."
Rap never liked being home alone.

The witch hollered, "Rap, heed my warning.
Better stay alone until the morning.
You know that you belong only to me.
Don't talk to no one. You're mine, you see."

The witch climbed down the stunning girl's locks
As I was jogging right down her block.
They call me Fine Prince. Everyone loves me.
There's no one who rises above me.

I looked up and saw the mean witch there.
Sliding right down some long silky hair.
The witch was yelling, "Rapunzel, see ya!
Be good or I . . . wouldn't wanna be ya!"

Then *poof!* the witch disappeared from sight.
The hair was pulled up to that great height.
I yelled, "Yo! Rapunzel!" and saw her face,
Then knew I had to get in that place.

I sang, "Rapunzel, let down your hair,
'Cause I'm so *fine,* we'd be a great pair."
She said, "Not now, Prince, maybe in a while.
I broke a nail. I've got to file."

I called again after an hour.
Her answer came down from the tower:
"I would love to see you. That's a sure bet.
But I've just shampooed. My hair's all wet."

I waited there but had to get in.
This hot, hot day was bad for my skin.
I heard her blow-dryer, drying away.
I sat and sat for most of the day.

Much later I called, "Drop your hair down."
Again her reply, it made me frown:
"You'll have to wait for a longer while
'Cause my hair's teased in a new def style."

When I saw her hair, "Oh no!" I said.
It shot straight up, way high, on her head.
There's no way that hair could be my ladder.
So, I sat . . . couldn't feel any sadder.

Two hours passed, then I heard the girl:
"This hair is lame. I've had it with curls.
I'll straighten it out, dress it with flowers.
It won't take long, just a few more hours."

I took a short nap there on the stoop,
When I awoke, was thrown for a loop.
There was Rapunzel, the girl of my dreams.
Down dropped her hair, so shiny it gleamed.

Climbing was rough. It took me a bit.
Her shrill whining was giving me fits.
"You're hurting my hair. When it twists and bends,
Your heavy weight will give me split ends."

Finally I made it up to her room.
I fell in love, but then heard a *kaboom!*
The mean witch was back and, man, she looked mad.
Her wand started smoking. This looked bad.

Next thing I knew I was zapped downtown
Where I didn't know my way around.
I was really lost, man. I'm not joking!
Then I pulled out my subway token.

I subwayed back to Rapunzel's place
But she'd disappeared without a trace.
I imagined the worst . . . bad to gory.
What happened next? Yo! Finish my story.

Rapunzel's Brush with Disaster and the Happy Split-Ending

After the witch zapped me out of her face,
She ran to Rapunzel, invaded her space.
She screamed, "I zap things to fill your every whim,
And when I come back, I find you with him!"

The witch got mad, then madder at the girl.
Rapunzel didn't care, sat twirling a curl.
"I'm glad you're back 'cause there's more stuff I need.
Like headphones, some sneakers," Rap said with greed.

Strange things happen when witches get that mad.
Their heads puff up big; that's when things turn real bad.
Rap then spoke again and blew the witch's mind:
"I never get anything!" young Rap whined.

Witch got so angry she overloaded
And all of a sudden her head exploded.
The blast shot dear Rapunzel out the window,
Hair cushioned her fall on the street below.

For weeks I searched the town for my dream girl.
Was wandering around when I noticed a curl.
"It looks like Rapunzel's!" I sang out with glee,
And followed the locks first one block, then three.

The locks led me to a hair-cutting place.
Inside snipped Rapunzel, a smile on her face.
I ran up to her and kissed her cheek so fair.
Then spat on the floor, my mouth filled with hair.

Rapunzel found her parents. That was good.
Then we all settled down, there in the hood.
Rap and I knew one thing—that's how to look fab.
We opened a shop that made beauties from drab.

Rap's hairstyles were a huge sensation.
Everyone had her look across the nation.
Kids, grown-ups, and even some teachers
Were looking cool with Rap's long-hair features.

But that wasn't how we got so happy.
We got all our kicks as a mom and pappy.
When Rapunzel gave birth to two kids, a pair—
A boy and a girl, with six feet of hair.

Rap was happy just styling their tresses,
In cornrows, dread locks, in curls or headdresses.
But out in the hood, Rap got all the stares.
That trendsetting girl had cut off all her hair.